Topsy + Tim

Buckets and Spades

Jean and Gareth Adamson

Ladybird

Early one morning, Dad called,
"Come along, tiddlers! We're ready
to start."

Published by Ladybird Books Ltd
27 Wrights Lane London W8 5TZ
A Penguin Company
3 5 7 9 10 8 6 4

First published MCMLXXXVIII © Jean and Gareth Adamson
This edition first published MCMXCIX
The moral rights of the author/artist have been asserted

Printed in Italy

Topsy and Tim ran to the car
carrying their buckets and spades.
They were going for a holiday at
the seaside.

First they drove to the garage to get the car ready for the journey. The garage man put the petrol in while Dad blew up the tyres.

"The windscreen could do with a wash," said Mummy.

Topsy and Tim fetched the water in their seaside buckets.

"All aboard," shouted Dad.

Tim waved to the garage man as they drove away.

"Goodbye everybody!" called Topsy.
"We're going to the seaside."

They buzzed along until the town was far behind. Then they had to slow right down behind a big, smelly lorry.

Suddenly Tim shouted, "We've left our buckets behind!"

"Never mind," said Mummy. "We'll
buy new buckets when we get there."

Tim began to cry. "I want my old
bucket," he sobbed.

"We're all getting hungry," said Mummy. "Let's stop and have a picnic."

Dad drove down a narrow country lane and pulled up by a farm gate. "Here's a good place for a picnic," he said.

Soon it was time to go.

"We must pick up all our litter," said Mummy.

"What shall we put it in?" asked Tim.

Mummy gave them an empty carrier bag for the litter.

"We could have put it in our good old seaside buckets," said Topsy.

Dad began to turn the car round.
Suddenly the back dropped down
with a bump.

"We've gone into the ditch," said
Dad.

Dad looked worried. "We need help," he said, "and here we are, miles from anywhere."

"I can hear a car," said Topsy.

The sound came nearer and stopped. Then a man looked over the hedge high above them.

"It's a friendly giant!" shouted Topsy and Tim.

The man wasn't a giant. He was sitting up in his tractor in the field behind the hedge. But he was friendly. He fixed a rope from his tractor to their car. Then the tractor tugged the car out of the ditch.

They drove on and soon came to
the top of a hill.

"I can see the sea!" shouted Topsy.

"I wish we had our old buckets,"
said Tim.

Soon they reached their holiday
village. Dad began to unload their
luggage.

"Hello!" he said. "What have I
found?"

"Our buckets!" shouted Topsy
and Tim.

They ran straight off to fill them
with seaside sand.

Match the colours.

Match the pairs.

How many buckets can you see?
How many seagulls?
How many boats?
How many children?

Tell the story.